88-91

An I Can Read Book®

Addie Meets Max

By Joan Robins

Pictures by Sue Truesdell

HarperTrophy®
A Division of HarperCollins*Publishers*

HarperCollins®, ®, Harper Trophy®, and I Can Read Book®
are trademarks of HarperCollins Publishers Inc.

Addie Meets Max

Library of Congress Cataloging-in-Publication Data
Robins, Joan
    Addie meets Max.
    (An I can read book)
    Summary: Addie discovers that the new boy next door,
Max, and his dog are not so terrible when she helps Max
bury his newly lost tooth.
    1. Children's stories, American. [1. Friendship—
Fiction] I. Truesdell, Sue, ill. II. Title. III. Series.
PZ7.R5555Ad   1984   [E]   84-48329
ISBN 0-06-025063-1
ISBN 0-06-025064-X (lib. bdg.)
ISBN 0-06-444116-4 (pbk.)

First Harper Trophy edition, 1988.
Designed by Al Cetta

to Quirk

Addie peeked over the fence.

"RUFF, RUFF," barked the dog.

Addie ran into the house.

"I saw the new boy next door.

He has a dog," said Addie.

"Did you say hello?"

asked Mother.

"I did *NOT*!" said Addie.

"His dog barked at me."

"Maybe the dog was saying hello,"

said Mother.

"It was not!" said Addie.

"It wanted me to go away."

7

The next day the boy

took a ride on his bike.

Addie saw him.

She got on her bike

and zoomed down the driveway.

"OOOOOOOOO!" cried the boy.

"OWWWWWWWW!" cried Addie.

Addie picked up her bike

and limped back to the house.

"Mother," she cried,

"he almost killed me."

"Who?" asked Mother.

"That new boy," said Addie.

"He ran into me with his bike.

Look!"

"Let me put a Band-Aid on it,"

said Mother.

"Two Band-Aids," said Addie.

"I want that boy

to move to the moon,

and stay there!"

"Nonsense," said Mother.

"His name is Max,

and he is coming for lunch today.

Maybe you will like him."

"Never ever!" cried Addie.

Addie ran to her room
and waited.

"Max is here, Addie,"

called Mother.

13

Addie went into the kitchen,

slowly.

"Max, this is Addie.

Addie, this is Max.

I know you both like pizza,"

said Mother.

15

Max ate and ate.

He did not say one word.

"Do you want more pizza?"

asked Addie.

Max shook his head.

16

"Do you like chocolate-chip cookies?"

asked Addie.

Max nodded his head.

Finally Addie said,

"Look what you did to me!"

Max looked at Addie's Band-Aids.

And he smiled.

"WOW!" cried Addie.

"You lost a tooth."

"It fell out when we crashed,"

said Max.

"Does it hurt?"

asked Addie.

"Not anymore," said Max.

"Does your leg hurt?"

"Not anymore," said Addie.

"What are you going to do

with your tooth?"

"Bury it," said Max.

"Do you want to help?"

Addie nodded her head.

"We can bury it

next to the fence,"

she said.

Max dug a deep hole

under the maple tree.

Addie sang,

"Good-bye tooth,

Good-bye tooth,

Max will miss you.

That's the truth."

"RUFF, RUFF, RUFF."

"EEEEEK!" cried Addie.

"It is only Ginger," said Max.

"She wants to say hello.

Look!"

Addie peeked over the fence.

Ginger was wagging her tail.

She tried to kiss Addie's nose.

Addie patted Ginger's soft ears.

"Oh, Max," she cried.

"Ginger likes me!"

Ginger ran behind the bushes.

She came back with a ball.

"She wants to play with us,"

said Max.

"YIPPEE!" cried Addie.

"Let's go!"